To: Evelyn.
Jene Nana.

Merry Xmas 2015.   XOXO

Just Grace and
the Double Surprise

Merry ~~Xmas~~

Xmas. Evelyn.
Jene Nana.
XOXO

Just Grace and the Double Surprise

Written and illustrated

by

Charise Mericle Harper

sandpiper

Houghton Mifflin Harcourt
Boston New York

All rights reserved. Published in the United States by Sandpiper, an imprint of
Houghton Mifflin Harcourt Publishing Company. Originally published in hardcover
in the United States by Houghton Mifflin Books for Children, an imprint of
Houghton Mifflin Harcourt Publishing Company, 2011.

SANDPIPER and the SANDPIPER logo are trademarks of Houghton Mifflin
Harcourt Publishing Company.

For information about permission to reproduce selections from this book,
write to Permissions, Houghton Mifflin Harcourt Publishing Company,
215 Park Avenue South, New York, New York 10003.

www.hmhbooks.com

The text of this book is set in Dante MT.
The illustrations are pen-and-ink drawings digitally colored by Photoshop.

The Library of Congress has cataloged the hardcover edition as follows:
Harper, Charise Mericle.
Just Grace and the double surprise / written and illustrated by Charise
Mericle Harper.
p. cm.
Summary: While Grace and her best friend Mimi are waiting for the arrival
of the baby sister Mimi's family plans to adopt, Grace gets a big surprise.
[1. Best friends—Fiction. 2. Friendship—Fiction. 3. Brothers and sisters—
Fiction. 4. Dogs—Fiction. 5. Schools—Fiction.] I. Title.
PZ7.H231323Jt 2011
[Fic]—dc23
2011015929

ISBN: 978-0-547-37026-2 hardcover
ISBN: 978-0-547-94219-3 paperback

Manufactured in the United States of America
DOC 10 9 8 7 6 5 4 3
4500406350

For all Just Grace fans new and old.
Thanks for reading!

THE BIG NEWS NEXT DOOR

Any day now Mimi, my best friend in the whole world, is going to be getting a brand-new sister. The minute the special phone call comes, Mimi and her parents are going to rush out the door, jump into their car, and drive off to get her. Mimi can't wait for that day to happen. It's very exciting.

Mimi said the waiting for the special call is making everyone at her house really jumpy, especially when the phone rings. That's why her mom has a new rule about me calling Mimi on the phone. The new rule is **don't call.** If I want to talk to Mimi I have to go over and knock on her front door—but this is only until the sister gets here. After that I get to use the phone again.

I want the big day to happen too. I don't like the waiting part. It's a new kind of waiting that I haven't known before—it's excited plus nervous plus worried plus happy all mixed together. And even though it's for something really good and great, it doesn't feel super comfortable.

SOME KINDS OF WAITING I KNOW

TYPES OF WAITING	FUN	NOT FUN
Sitting in a doctor's office.		Usually the books and magazines are torn up and old, and the crayons for drawing are all bad colors.
In line at the grocery store.	If I am with Dad—he lets me touch stuff.	If I am with Mom—she doesn't want me to touch stuff.
Waiting for my food in a restaurant.	We always play I-spy, and I am excellent at that game.	
Waiting for Mom or Dad to finish what they are doing so they can help me with something.		This always seems to take forever, even though they say, "I'll just be a minute."

WHAT I KNOW ABOUT LITTLE KIDS

Mom said that when kids are little their brains are like brand-new sponges—everything they see or hear soaks up into their brain and then stays up there forever. That's why kids are so good at learning new stuff—their brain-sponges are new. When a sponge is new it's really soft and excellent at holding stuff. When a sponge is old and used up it doesn't work so well anymore. Grown-up brains are like old sponges—they are worn out and can't pick stuff up very well, plus they are already pretty full. Sometimes even too full to hold anything new—like when Mom forgot my fifty cents for bake sale day, even though I probably re-minded her about it three, four, or even five times.

NO FAIR! EVERYONE ELSE GETS TO HAVE COOKIES AND CUPCAKES!

← APPLE THAT WAS PACKED IN MY LUNCH BY MOM.

NO MONEY IN POCKETS →

WHAT WOULD BE A GOOD SCIENCE FAIR PROJECT

SPONGES AND BRAINS

★ THIS WILL BE THE WINNER!

WHO LEARNS MORE?
(THE BRAIN-SPONGE TEST)

YOUNG PERSON★

OLD PERSON

Ⓐ

Ⓑ

1. TAKE SPONGE AND LET IT SOAK UP LIQUID FROM THE BOWL.

2. SQUEEZE OUT SPONGE IN MEASURING CUP.

3. REPEAT FOR Ⓑ SPONGE.

4. WHICH CUP HAS MORE LIQUID?

BRAND-NEW SPONGE

OLD WORN-OUT SPONGE

Ⓐ   Ⓑ

←BOWLS→

Ⓐ   ←MEASURING CUPS→   Ⓑ

WHAT I NEEDED TO DO RIGHT AWAY

If Mimi's sister's brain was like a sponge, then
I had to make sure it was going to suck up
and remember my Grace name and not my

Just Grace name by accident. I did not want the wrong name to be staying in her head forever. That's why I got the idea to make her a book as a welcome-to-your-new-family present. I went to the library a couple of times to do research on books for little kids.

Because I like books, I was already knowing two things about kids' books:

1. My book for Mimi's sister had to be short.

2. It had to have pictures on every page.

Moms like to read short books at bedtime, so it was good that I was thinking about that part before I even got started. I bet if Mimi's mom read my book to the new sister even just eight or ten times, that was going to be enough for it to work perfectly. Mimi's new sister would never forget my real name.

After visiting the library I was hoping that Mimi's sister was not going to be like the kids that were in there when I was doing my book research. Those kinds of kids should only be allowed to touch special books—books that can't be destroyed by eating, drooling, or ripping. My book was just going to be paper and cardboard. I was a little worried about that.

DROOLING ON BOOK

RIPPING BOOK

CUTE HAT THOUGH

TRYING TO EAT BOOK

LOOKING INTO THE FUTURE

I was writing the book for Mimi's sister so that I could solve the problem of Mimi's new sister calling me Just Grace before it even ever happened. This kind of thinking is called advance planning. I learned this from Mom. She is a pretty good what-could-happen-in-the-future thinker. Mostly she does her best work when we are going on a trip: she remembers snacks, water, tissues, extra clothes, and all that kind of stuff. She's not as good with regular everyday things. I think she gets lazy unless it's a special occasion.

WHAT IS KIND OF HARD

Writing a little kid's picture book is not as easy as you would think it would be. Mostly that's because this kind of book is not suppose to have a lot of words in it. It's surprising, but the hardest part is deciding which words to take out so that only the most important ones are left over. I think a book with more words might be easier.

THINGS I WANTED TO SAY IN MY BOOK

I wanted to explain how I got the Just Grace

name from Miss Lois, our teacher, and how it was all a big accident. There are three other Graces in our class and Miss Lois thought it would be too confusing if we all kept our names like they were. She said we needed new names, so we could know whose attention she wanted if she called out the name Grace. Her big idea was to put the first initial of our last name at the end of our Grace name. I don't think anyone really liked it, but you can't argue with a teacher, because at school they mostly get to be the boss.

Since I was last in line for a new name I had the better idea to just be called Grace.

And because no one else was using just **Grace,** it seemed perfect . . . but it wasn't!

Miss Lois obviously gets confused really easily. I wonder if it would have been different if I had said *only* Grace instead? Or maybe Only Grace would have become my new name.

CHILDREN'S BOOKS CAN BE SNEAKY

Some children's books have lessons mixed in with the fiction part of the story. This is a good way to get little kids to learn stuff without even knowing they are learning.

I wanted my lesson to be "Even though you think you have a perfect plan, other people can still mess it up." I tried to fit it into the story, but I think it was too important and big for a little picture book—it's probably more of a chapter book thing, and I am not ready to write one of those!

MY BOOK

This is your sister, Mimi.

Mimi is great!

This is your house.

Mimi lives in the house.

This is the house next to your house.

GRACE lives in this house.

GRACE is nice.

GRACE and Mimi are friends.

GRACE is waving bye-bye.
It's time for GRACE to go home.

This is Crinkles. He is a cat.

Cats are dangerous!!!!!

WHAT I AM WORRIED ABOUT NOW

Writing the book solved my Just Grace problem, but when I was working on it I suddenly thought of a new problem. Crinkles! How were we going to keep Mimi's new sister away from him? Mimi is completely allergic to cats. If you pet a cat and then stand next to Mimi her body will totally know it. In about twenty seconds she will start sneezing. It's like she has superpowers for detecting cat germs.

ITCHY EYES

HAVE YOU TOUCHED A CAT?

THAT'S AMAZING! HOW DID YOU KNOW?

Little kids love cats and dogs. The new sister will probably be touching Crinkles all the time. She will be a walking furball, and Mimi will have to stay away from her. Poor Mimi. Maybe the new sister would believe my story about Crinkles being a biting cat. I'm pretty sure if you write something that's not true in a picture book it doesn't count as a lie.

PLAY WITH ME, MIMI!

I CAN'T COME ANY CLOSER! MY EYES AND MY THROAT ARE SO ITCHY!

NEW SISTER COVERED IN CRINKLES'S FUR

WHAT CAN HAPPEN IF YOU ARE NOT CAREFUL

Once you are worrying about one thing, you can start thinking about all the other things that you could worry about too. It's like there is suddenly a bridge into your brain and all the worries decide to run over it at the same time.

If this happens, the best thing to do is to get up and go do something else. Sitting and thinking just keeps the bridge open. Moving around can sometimes destroy it.

WHAT HAPPENED NEXT

I went downstairs to the kitchen to see what Mom was doing. I heard rustling and talking, so it sounded like maybe she and Dad were having a snack—I hoped it was a cookies snack. As soon as I walked into the kitchen they both looked up and stopped talking. When parents do this it usually means they have been talking about you.

"What are you talking about?" I asked. I knew they would probably not really tell me. "We were talking about you," said Mom. I was 100 percent surprised. That was not the answer I was expecting. Normally Mom makes up something boring so she thinks I won't guess it was about me. Something like, "We were discussing how the toilet paper rolls seem to have gotten smaller," or "Your father was telling me about the exciting new W611 form he had to fill out for work." Basically the kind of stuff I would never in a million years care about. This telling the truth was something I was not ready for. Maybe I was about to get in trouble. This got my brain thinking: *What could it be? What did I do wrong?*

WHAT YOU CAN DO IF YOU ARE ABOUT TO GET INTO TROUBLE

Before your mom or dad can even say one word about anything, start apologizing—they seem to get less mad if the "I'm sorry" part comes before the "We are so angry with you" part. I picked the first bad thing I could think of and said, "I'm really sorry. I know you bought me that new purple shirt, but the arms were too tight and it didn't look good. I tried to wear it—really I did. Even Mimi thought it was kind of ugly. I'm sorry. I'll never throw a shirt away again. I promise." That was a lot to say and I was hoping it was working, but I couldn't really tell because I was looking at the floor. If you do something bad you should always look at the floor—it makes you look sadder and more filled with sorry feelings.

"You threw away your new purple shirt?" Mom sounded surprised. This was not good.

Now I had apologized for something they didn't even know about yet. Mistake apologies are the worst!

HOW TV SAVED MY LIFE

Mom was not happy. I could tell because she was making her I-don't-like-what-I'm-hearing face that makes her forehead all wrinkled. This face always comes with lots of questions. "What was wrong with it? I thought it was cute. Why didn't you say something before I cut the tags off?" She was sounding less surprised and more and more upset. I tried to explain, "I'm sorry. I thought I liked it, but then when I tried it on . . ." I wanted to say, ". . . it looked super ugly," but I knew that would make things worse so I said, "it wasn't . . . flattering." Most eight-year-olds probably wouldn't know that word, but I learned it from TV. It's a nice way to say your outfit looks horrible. Mom and I sometimes watch *Dress Your Best* on TV and they use that word whenever someone looks bad in their outfit. It's a good word because it doesn't hurt people's feelings.

THIS HURTS FEELINGS

ALL THOSE STRIPES MAKE YOU LOOK LIKE A GIANT ZEBRA.

YOU'RE SO MEAN! NOW I'M SAD.

THIS DOES NOT HURT FEELINGS

WHAT WAS AMAZING

It worked! Mom smiled and shook her head and looked at Dad. Dad doesn't care about fashion. He'll pretty much wear anything Mom buys for him. He looked at us both and shrugged his shoulders. "Well, I hope it's still in the garbage," said Mom. "Someone will be happy to have a perfectly good shirt. I'll wash it and we can donate it."

"Thank you! Thank you! Thank you, TV!" I said this inside my head so no one else could hear it. I was so happy. I didn't even wait for Mom to ask me to get the shirt. I ran straight outside to the garbage can. "I'll get it," I yelled back.

Sometimes avoiding disaster can feel like a gift. You're worried and scared you'll get into trouble and then when it doesn't happen your insides suddenly feel brand new.

WHAT WAS LUCKY

The ugly purple shirt was still in the garbage can.

WHAT WAS UNLUCKY

The ugly purple shirt was underneath some slimy paper towels, which I had to touch with my bare hands to get it out. YUCK!

WHAT I WAS THINKING NOW

I really, really, really, really, really, hate you, purple shirt!

How I Knew Mom Wasn't Mad Anymore

After I dropped the shirt onto the laundry pile I went back to the kitchen, and there, on a plate in the middle of the table, were two snicker-doodle cookies. They didn't have my name on them but I could tell they were for me.

It wasn't until I was halfway through cookie number two that I started thinking and wondering about the whole Mom and Dad talking thing again. Why were they talking about me? Why would they admit it? What was going on? I had a feeling it wasn't something bad, so for sure I wasn't going to apologize about Mom's lipstick unless she brought it up first.

BROKEN

LIPSTICK IS NOT AS STRONG AS YOU WOULD GUESS IT WOULD BE. IT DOES NOT WORK VERY WELL AS A CRAYON.

I'm not good at guessing what's in Mom and Dad's brain, so all I could do was hope—hope for something good! Lately there's a lot of hoping going on in my life, and I'm getting kind of good at it.

WHAT MIMI AND I ARE HOPING

We know it will never happen, but if you are going to spend energy wishing you should probably wish for a whole pie and not just a little piece of pie.

OUR WISH PIE

Mimi decided that the perfect age for the new sister is three years old. That way there will be no diapers, she can talk, she can play and do stuff, and she is still small enough to be picked up. Mimi really wants a sister she can carry around. The only bad part about a three-year-old sister is that she is for sure going to already have a name. Mimi's mom said that if the sister was not a baby they would probably have to keep the name she came with. It could be anything, even a name like Helga or Mildred, but Mimi and I are using all our energy to hope for a Jasmine. We looked at hundreds of sister names and it's our favorite.

WHAT YOU CAN'T DO

Adopting a new sister is not like shopping in a grocery store. You can't just look at all the kids and then point to the one you want. Mimi said there are special people who decide which families should get which children. They don't want to make a mistake and put the wrong kid in the wrong family—that's why the whole thing takes so long. I don't really understand how it all works, but we have some adopted kids at school and they seem happy so I guess the decider people know how to do it right.

WHAT I DIDN'T TELL MIMI

I was thinking that even if the sister was named something else maybe we could train her to like the Jasmine name better. It could start off as sort of a nickname, and then when she was knowing it really well, we could make the switch. Right now Mimi was really worried about doing stuff wrong and then not getting to have a sister at all, so I decided it was better to not tell her about the idea until later.

WHAT I DID RIGHT BEFORE BED

Mimi and I always flash our lights on and off at each other before we go to sleep. Our bedroom windows are right across from each other so it's perfect. Usually we just flash our lights a couple of times and then that's it, but lately Mimi wants us each to do it an exact number of times: one flash for each letter in the word *sister*. She says it's for luck. I haven't asked her but I bet she spells out *sister* when she does her flashes. I just count to six—it's easier.

ME

MIMI

We did our flashes and then right before I jumped in bed I put Chip-Up in his little bed next to me on the floor. I don't know why, but I have been deciding to do that lately. Chip-Up's the pretend dog I made hoping that Mom and Dad would get the hint and let me have a real dog. It didn't work so well. At first I was really disappointed, but then I kind of got over it. I guess we're just not a pet kind of family. I'm pretty happy with how Chip-Up turned out. Some- times at night, if I wake up sleepy and look down at him, he almost looks real.

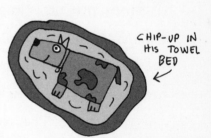

CHIP-UP IN HIS TOWEL BED

THE BREAKFAST OF MYSTERY

Dad wasn't at the table when I got down to breakfast. He doesn't usually leave for work until after I leave for school. I asked Mom just to be sure. "Is Dad gone? Did he have a meeting?" He had forgotten to say goodbye, which was also really weird. "Oh, honey, he was late for the train and you were in the bathroom," said Mom. "He shouted good-bye, but you must not have heard him. I'm sorry." "He could have tried harder," I mumbled. This was not starting out as a good day. I don't like it when things are different by surprise.

Mom tried to cheer me up by being all smiley. Then she said, "Oh, I almost forgot. Your father is coming home early today, so hurry home from school. He's taking you on an errand." The word *errand* is never for something good. It almost always means having to go somewhere that is boring and not fun. "Do I have to? I bet it's the dumb hardware store." Now I was grumpy.

"Yes, you have to go," said Mom. "Plus I think you're going to like it." She had a big smile on her face that instantly made a giant invisible question mark pop up right above my head.

WHAT MOM IS EXCELLENT AT

"What? What is it? Tell me! Tell me! Where are we going?" I was jumping up and down and filled with need-to-know energy. I 100 percent wanted to know what she was talking about, but Mom just smiled and turned around. "You'll have to wait and see," she said. Mom is probably one of the best secret keepers in the whole entire world. It's not easy being her daughter. I had tried before so I knew that if she said no, there was no way she was going to change her mind. Asking her over and over again was not going to work. Mom would never tell. The best thing to do was to try and stop thinking about the secret. This is not easy.

Mom was making my lunch so I made myself ask her about that instead. "What am I having today?" "Turkey and cheese," said Mom. This was not an exciting answer. "Turkey and cheese again?" I stuck my tongue out. "But you love turkey and cheese," said Mom. She was right—I did—but having the same lunch every day was getting boring. I wanted lunch to be fun. I wanted my lunch bag to be full of little surprise packages—each one filled with something new and exciting to eat—like presents for my mouth.

"Well, how about a jam sandwich?" asked Mom. Ugh—jam was boring too. "No, I guess I'll just have the turkey and cheese." I slouched in my chair. "I'll cut it in four pieces," said Mom. "That'll make it more fun." I could tell she was smiling at her own joke. When you know someone, even if you can't see their face, you can still tell if they are smiling while talking. Smiling makes a voice sound different.

THE WALK TO SCHOOL

I was ready a little early, so I walked across the yard to get Mimi. These days Mimi doesn't like to leave for school until the last possible second. She wants to wait as long as she can just in case the sister people call. Yesterday we had to run the last two blocks just to make it before the second bell. I'm hoping things are going to go back to normal once the sister gets here.

I was talking to Mom about it yesterday, but she said not to get my hopes up about everything being normal anytime soon. She said it was going to take a while for Mimi to adjust to a new sister. I'm hoping she is wrong. I like normal.

WHY WE DID NOT WALK TO SCHOOL

Okay. It's official. Mimi is going a little crazy. When I got to her house she said I should go back home and put my sneakers on. "Let's run to school," said Mimi. "Because it's good exercise." Of course I was right away knowing that she didn't want to run to school for exercise. She wanted to run to school so that she could have more time at home waiting for the phone to ring.

If she wasn't my best friend I would have said, "See you at school," and walked on without her, but she *is* my best friend, so I went home and changed my shoes. I'm not so big on getting all sweaty first thing in the morning, but by the time Mimi's mom made us leave we didn't have a choice—we had to run.

I tried to tell Mimi about my breakfast mystery but it was hard to run and talk at the same time.

Finally I just had to say, "Oh, forget it!"

WHAT IS NOT GOOD TO HEAR

While I was walking to my seat Robert Walters said, "Ewww! Why are you so sweaty?" I gave him a be-quiet look but he didn't care—he kept right on talking. "What? I was only asking, 'cause it's kind of gross." Right then I was hating Robert Walters more than I hated the purple shirt, and I hated the purple shirt a lot!

WHAT CAN MAKE ALL BAD FEELINGS GO AWAY SUPER FAST

Sometimes words can be just like a magic wand. I know magic wands don't really exist—as in, there is no such thing as a stick with magic powers—but still, there are things that have wandlike powers.

BEFORE THE MAGIC

THE MAGIC

CLASS, I HAVE A MEETING THIS MORNING.

MR. FRANK IS GOING TO BE HERE AS YOUR SUBSTITUTE WHILE I AM OUT.

AFTER

WHAT MAKES A THIRD GRADE CLASS SUDDENLY BURST INTO APPLAUSE

As soon as Mr. Frank walked in the door Owen 1 started clapping. About two seconds later everyone else joined in too. It was like Mr. Frank was a celebrity or something. We were all just so happy to see him—we couldn't help it. I think he and Miss Lois were both really surprised. Even though sometimes Miss Lois is not always my favorite teacher I hope she was not thinking that we were clapping because she was leaving. It wasn't true, but I could see how maybe she might be thinking that. It would have been good if someone had shouted, "Please, Miss Lois, we want you to stay too!" I looked at Sunni because she was the only one who would probably say that—she is Miss Lois's favorite student. But she had her hand up, trying to get Mr. Frank's attention instead.

Even if your brain thinks of something that would be good to do, it doesn't mean your body will do that thing. I looked at Miss Lois, but my mouth just couldn't say the words. I felt better after she and Mr. Frank whispered something to each other and both smiled. Maybe she didn't feel bad after all. Sometimes my empathy power can really get in the way of everyday life.

EMPATHY POWER: THE ABILITY TO TELL HOW OTHER PEOPLE ARE FEELING.

I CAN ONLY BE HAPPY WHEN EVERYONE AROUND ME IS TRULY HAPPY.

THIS IS NOT AN EASY POWER TO LIVE WITH.

WHAT HAPPENED NEXT

Craziness!!!

WHY

Everyone wanted to talk to Mr. Frank at the same time. It had been forever since we had last seen him, and so we all had to tell him about the new stuff in our lives. Some people had more interesting new stuff than other people. Owen 1 being able to make a basketball go into the hoop with one eye closed was not anywhere as exciting or as important as Mimi getting a new sister.

Finally Mr. Frank had to ask everyone to stop talking at the same time. Even though he is more fun than Miss Lois, he still uses some of the same teacher sayings she does. It's probably the kind of thing they both learned at teacher school.

TEACHER SAYINGS

I NEED EVERYONE'S ATTENTION AT
    THE FRONT.

BOTTOMS IN YOUR CHAIRS, EVERYONE.

SETTLE DOWN, CLASS.

I STILL HEAR SOME TALKING.

LET'S HAVE ALL EYES ON ME.

You don't hear these kind of sentences unless you are sitting in a classroom.

WHAT IS SURPRISINGLY FUN TO DO

We have been learning a lot about geography and maps. At first I did not think that this was going to be very interesting, but Miss Lois has been working hard to make the boring parts more fun. So far my favorite part has been legends. A legend on a map is not the same as a legend that is in a story.

STORY LEGEND

MAP LEGEND

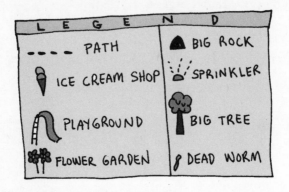

Map legends help you understand maps—they are like the clues so you can know what you are looking at when you read a map. Miss Lois had us do a map of our classroom and we got to use all sorts of crazy stuff in our legends. I used buttons for the chairs, Mimi used star stickers, but the weirdest one was Sammy—he used little pieces of chewed-up gum. I thought for sure he was going to get in trouble, but he didn't. Miss Lois said it was disgusting and she didn't want to touch it, but she let him hang it up in the hallway next to all the other class maps. I think everyone was pretty surprised about that.

WHAT WE HAVE TO DO

Mr. Frank said we have to use our map skills to make a map. It can be a map of anywhere or anything we want, but it has to be of something real. At first the class was really excited, but then people started to groan and complain that they didn't know what to do. "I don't have any ideas," said Sunni. This was really unusual because Sunni always knows exactly what to do. I think the fact that Sunni was stuck confused everyone else. If the superstar of the class didn't know what to do, how were we, the regular students, supposed to know what to do? The only person who had an idea was Robert Walters. "I am going to make a map of my bathroom," said Roger. He stood up, waved his pencil in the air, and then sat back down again. Like that was going to help anyone—plus, who was going to want to see that map anyway!

WHAT IS WRONG WITH MR. FRANK

Mr. Frank thinks we are better and smarter than we really are. We are just a bunch of kids, but sometimes I think he forgets that. Kids need help deciding stuff, because they have amazing imaginations. It's hard to believe, but sometimes having too much imagination or too many choices can make it hard to decide what to do.

Deciding can be easier when there are not a lot of choices.

Make a map of anything you can think of:

Make a map of your kitchen:

WHAT MR. FRANK DID NOT WANT

Mr. Frank did not want us all to be making the same map. He said we should feel creative and playful. Then, to help us start feeling those things, he gave us a list of unusual map ideas.

THINGS YOU CAN MAKE A MAP OF

1. Your kitchen table at breakfast, lunch, and dinner.

2. Your walk to school.

3. A room in your house.

4. Your favorite playground.

5. Your front yard and how it changes with the seasons.
6. Your dog's favorite walk.

WHAT HAPPENED NEXT

I could tell that most of the class was starting to feel better about the project. It can be easier to think of an idea if you get a little push in the right direction. Of course some kids picked stuff right off the list, but not everyone did. Mr. Frank was especially happy with the people who were coming up with their own new original ideas.

I'M GOING TO MAKE A MAP OF MY CAT'S FAVORITE SLEEPING SPOTS.

I'M GOING TO MAKE A MAP OF THE BEST PLACES TO HIDE CANDY IN MY HOUSE.

Mimi decided to draw a map of all the fun places to play in her yard, and what games you could play where. I knew she was making it for the new sister. Even though three-year-olds probably can't read maps, she could for sure save it for the sister until she got older. I wanted to think of something interesting and original. I wanted Mr. Frank to be proud of me too.

I had lots of thoughts in my head and not one of them was a good idea.

But then . . .

MAP OF ME

Sometimes when you have a great idea your brain suddenly feels like a huge fireworks show, with hundreds of different thoughts exploding all at once.

My brain was thinking, "Oh my gosh! I can't believe I just thought of this! This is the best idea ever! YAY!!!! Wow!!!! I am totally going to do this! I am so excited!" And with all this going on in my head, it just seemed crazy that the whole class could not be noticing it, because for me it felt so big and so everything! I looked around, but everyone was just quietly working away. Sammy looked up for a second, but it was obvious he couldn't tell that my head was almost exploding.

WHAT IS TRUE

If you are waiting for something, time goes by really slowly. If you are not waiting and instead you are having fun, time goes by really fast. It seemed like only two seconds had gone by and then Mr. Frank said it was time for lunch—about half the class groaned. This kind of thing must make teachers super happy. Mostly kids want to get away from schoolwork, not stay and do more. It's the kind of thing a teacher would for sure write in their journal if they kept one.

Today was the best day EVER!!! The kids wanted to stay in the classroom instead of going outside to play. I really am a good teacher!!!

MY MAP SO FAR

HEART THAT FEELS WHEN OTHER PEOPLE ARE SAD.

FROM FALLING OFF BENCH AT THE PARK WHEN A WASP WAS FLYING AROUND MY HEAD BECAUSE IT WANTED TO EAT MY ICE CREAM.

← FROM FALLING OFF MY BIKE. (IT IS NOT SAFE TO RIDE FAST OVER TOP OF WET LEAVES.)

LEGEND
* SCAR

Mr. Frank said we would have to finish our map projects at home. After lunch Miss Lois was coming back and he was leaving to go upstairs and be an afternoon substitute for a fifth grade class. The class groaned again, but this time it was for a totally different reason.

WHAT I WAS NOT EXPECTING

"Hey, that's a great idea. Can I do that too?" Those words were from Sammy, and they were a surprise. He was standing right beside me, looking at my map. I was in such a good mood and so happy that without even thinking about it I said, "Sure." That was a surprise too. My mouth surprised my brain. If my mouth had not moved so fast my brain might have thought to say, "No, that's my idea. Think of your own." But it was too late. "Thanks," said Sammy, and he walked off. Well, his map is going to be nothing like mine. Both my brain and my mouth were happy and sure about that.

WHAT WAS SURPRISING AT LUNCH

Even though I was having turkey and cheese AGAIN, for like the six hundredth time, it tasted amazingly delicious. It was almost the best turkey and cheese sandwich I had ever had in my whole entire life. For sure it was not because Mom had cut it into four pieces, but there was *something* extra good about it.

WHAT MIMI SAID

At lunch Mimi and I talked about our maps. I couldn't believe she was already finished with hers. "How can you be done? I still have tons to do!" I didn't mean to, but I was kind of complaining. "I always pick simple things," said Mimi. "You like to make things more complicated. You think more than I do." "No, I don't," I said. "Everyone thinks the same. I mean, they think about different stuff, but the thinking part is the same, right?" I had never thought about this before. See! That is proof. I'm not always thinking.

"No, I don't think so," said Mimi. "You're definitely more of a thinker than me. Sometimes I don't even think about anything." "Really?" I said. "You can think about nothing?" I couldn't believe it. My brain is a nonstop chatterbox. I thought all brains were like that.

Suddenly one of the lunch ladies was yelling. "Did you throw that carrot? You! You in the blue shirt." She was pointing at a boy and her face was turning red. It was a nice break from all the thinking about thinking, because that kind of thinking was giving me a headache.

WHAT HAPPENED AFTER LUNCH

Miss Lois came back and we had to do our regular learning stuff. Even though it was Sunni who asked if we could work on our maps instead, she still said no. We were all hoping Sunni could convince her, but being a teacher's pet doesn't seem to give you extra power over a teacher's brain.

REALLY SMART BRAIN.

EARS ARE ALWAYS LISTENING.

* STILL CANNOT CONTROL TEACHER WITH HER EYES.

MOUTH ALWAYS SAYS THE RIGHT THING.

HOMEWORK IS DONE PERFECTLY.

PENCIL IS NEVER MISSING.

* TOO BAD!

WHAT WAS OKAY

The afternoon went by pretty quick, and that was because I was using my After Lunch Plan. I got the idea from Miss Lois's new way of getting Robert Walters to behave better. Robert loves baseball, so Miss Lois made a rule that each time he does something wrong it's called a strike. He is allowed to get two misbehave strikes in the morning and two misbehave strikes in the afternoon. If he gets three in either the morning or the afternoon it's called a strikeout, and then he has to go down the hall to visit with Mr. Harris. Mr. Harris is the principal, and it is not fun to have a talk with him in his office.

So far Miss Lois's plan seems to be working. She must be happy about that. I am using Miss Lois's plan too, but she hasn't noticed. Every afternoon right after Robert gets his first strike I ask to either go to the bathroom or get a drink of water. Taking little breaks from being in the classroom really makes the afternoon time go by a lot faster. I'm lucky that our class is such a busy place. It makes it harder for Miss Lois to notice what I'm doing.

REASONS TO GET OUT OF YOUR SEAT

1. Feel sick.
2. Have to go to the bathroom.

3. Need a drink of water.
4. Need a tissue.
5. Have to sharpen a pencil.
6. Finished work and need to get a silent reading book.
7. Have to talk to a friend about something—this one usually gets a "NO. Wait until after class."

WHAT MIMI WANTED TO DO WHEN THE BELL RANG

Since I was supposed to hurry straight home from school it was nice that Mimi was ready to go too. "Want to run?" she asked. I did not want to run with my big heavy backpack. "No, let's just walk fast," I said. "I bet we can still get there quick." Mimi seemed okay with that. I could tell she was dying to get home to see if they were going to go and pick up the new sister. I had never thought about it before, but what if this was not going to stop? What if even when the new sister got here Mimi was going to be rushing home every day to see her? What if Mimi was changing forever and not just for a little while like I thought she was? What if everything was going to be different?

I looked at Mimi for clues but I couldn't tell anything—she looked over and smiled. But Mimi is not like me. She doesn't have empathy power. She couldn't tell that my insides were not the same as my outsides. She couldn't feel my wondering about her. "Thanks for walking fast," she said. "It's okay," I said. "I have to get home quick too." And then I finally told her about the mystery breakfast.

THE MYSTERY IS A SURPRISE

A mystery is something you don't know the answer to. Sometimes there are clues to help you, but still, that doesn't mean you will ever find the answer. Some mysteries are never solved.

A surprise is kind of like a mystery because it has the same not-knowing-something part, but with a surprise you will always find out the answer if you wait long enough—the hard part is the waiting. Sometimes surprises have clues. I was going to keep my eyes open in case I could notice some.

Mimi and I said goodbye at the sidewalk, she ran to her front door and I walked to mine. As soon as I put my hand on the doorknob Dad stepped out and said, "Ready to go?" Wow! He really was excited to get going.

I was surprised. "Uh, okay," I said. I dropped my backpack and turned around. Dad smiled and pointed to the car.

Clue Number One: We were going to drive there.

From the car I could see my backpack sitting on the front steps. That kind of thing always gets Mom upset. She likes things to be put away. "Oops—my backpack," I said, but Dad was already backing out of the driveway. "Oh, it's fine," he said. "Your mother can pick it up." Well, Dad was going to have to get into trouble for that one, not me.

WHY I LIKE DRIVING WITH DAD

Dad always puts the music on really loud.

WHAT DAD IS NOT

Dad is not a good secret keeper. He is not like Mom. He likes to give lots of clues, and sometimes if he is not careful, his clues are too easy. "So, where are we going?" I shouted. I had to shout because the music was so loud. Dad turned down the music and said, "Hmm, let's see if I can think of some clues for you." While he was thinking, I was glad that we drove right by the hardware store. I was happy the surprise was not going to come from in there!

UNEXCITING THINGS FROM THE HARDWARE STORE

BUCKET

ROPE

CLEANING STUFF

SCREWS

DAD'S CLUES

- Bigger than a shoe
- Smaller than a horse
- Cute

These were not helpful clues!

"Oh, Daddy! That's too hard. It could be anything." I used my little-girl voice, because sometimes it makes Dad feel sorry for me. It doesn't work on Mom—it just makes her sigh and roll her eyes. "Sorry, little girl, that's all I'm allowed to say." Dad put his finger to his lips and said, "I'm under strict orders from the chief." Darn it! That meant that Mom had gotten to Dad and told him not to tell me anything. I was going to complain about Mom, but just then we turned onto the lane for the highway.

Clue Number Two: We were heading out of town.

WHAT IS FRUSTRATING ABOUT GUESSING

Mostly it's that one person knows the answer and the other person doesn't. It's not so bad with parents. At least it was Dad who had the secret. It's much worse when the secret holder is a kid.

PARENT SECRET HOLDER

KID SECRET HOLDER

Dad turned the music back up and I tried to just look out the window and not think about it.

WHAT WAS IMPOSSIBLE

NOT THINKING ABOUT IT!

FINALLY

After what seemed like forever, or maybe twenty minutes, Dad said, "Okay, we're almost there." I looked around for clues. You would think that if you were super close to a surprise you would be able to see lots of big clues. Well, if you were thinking this you would be wrong! I saw a gas station, lots of grass, a power line thing, and a farm with three muddy black cows—nothing looked very cluelike or interesting.

WHAT DAD SAID NEXT

"Now listen: I know you are going to be excited! But I want you to try to be calm. Okay? Will you try to remember that?" "Yeah, sure, Dad." Now I was really confused and excited and nervous and basically almost not able to sit still. And then we pulled into a driveway and I saw it—the sign that was the biggest clue of all.

Clue Number Three: A sign that said OAKLEY ANIMAL SHELTER.

"Let's go meet our new friend," said Dad. I couldn't speak. I knew what I wanted to be true, but I was scared it wasn't going to be what I was hoping for. I didn't want to be disappointed. "Are you okay?" asked Dad. I was standing by the car, but my feet were stuck. "I thought you wanted a dog?" said Dad. He sounded worried. "Oh, Daddy!" I cried. "Thank you! Thank you! Thank you!" Real tears were filling up my eyes—I couldn't stop them. I wiped my eyes and said, "I was worried that maybe it was going to be a turtle or something." Dad hugged me and said, "Would I drive for forty minutes to pick up a turtle? So what do you think? Should we go inside?" I blew my nose and nodded a big yes.

WHAT IS VERY NOISY

A barn full of dogs.

WHAT IS SAD

Dad said I could go and look at the dogs while he spoke to the people at the front desk. There were so many dogs, and they all seemed so excited to see me. As soon as I walked by their cages they ran to the front and started barking. I can't speak Dog, but I felt like they were saying, "Pick me! Pick me! Take me home. I want to be your new best friend." There were so many lonely dogs, I was never going to be able to choose one.

WHAT HAPPENED NEXT

"Come here, Grace," said Dad. He was at the end of the hall. He pointed to a door with a window in it and said, "Look in there." I peeked into the room, and there standing next to a lady in a white coat was the cutest little dog ever. "What do you think?" asked Dad. "Do you like her? Do you want to meet her? You can go in." As soon as I stepped into the room the little white dog ran up to me. I kneeled down and—surprise!—she jumped right into my lap. "Ahhh!" I fell back on the floor. "Oh, dear—are you okay?" asked the lady in the coat. "I think she's fine," said Dad, and he was right. I was happy on the inside, happy on the outside, and hardly worried at all about how clean the floor was.

WHAT CAN HAPPEN

Can a girl suddenly fall in love in two seconds? Can a girl suddenly love her parents more in the afternoon than she thought she did in the morning? Can a girl be happy with a new friend even if she did not pick out that new friend herself?

The answer to all these questions is yes.

MY NEW DOG

I love my new dog! The only not-good thing about her is her name. It's Mr. Scruffers! When Dad first told me I said, "What? She's not a boy! She's not a mister. That's a stupid name." Dad said, "Grace, don't say stupid. I'm sure you can change her name—she's only a year old." We were driving home and my new dog was lying almost perfectly in my lap. She was a little bigger so her legs were kind of falling off, but she seemed happy.

I was glad that Dad had picked her out. It would have been too hard and sad for me to do the picking.

Dad said he'd spent a long time talking to the people at the shelter, and when Mr. Scruffers arrived they called him right away. I'm glad it was a short surprise and that I didn't know anything about it until almost the end. It would have been hard to know I was getting a dog and then have to wait and wait and wait for the perfect one to get there.

WHAT DAD TALKED ABOUT ALL THE WAY HOME

Being a responsible dog owner.

WHAT I THOUGHT ABOUT ALL THE WAY HOME

I can't wait to show Mimi my dog.

What should her new name be?

I hope she wants to sleep on my bed with me.

WHAT I SAW WHEN I GOT HOME

Mom was sitting on the front steps. That was unusual, so I knew she was waiting for us. I jumped out of the car and we ran up to meet her. My new dog was really good on the leash. "Let's see this Mr. Scruffers," said Mom. "Oh! She is just the cutest thing!" Mom was petting and hugging her.

"I'm not going to keep calling her Mr. Scruffers," I said. "I'm going to think of something better." "Hmm," said Mom. "How about Cleo, or Millie, or . . . oh, I don't know. I'm sure you'll come up with something." Mom wanted to keep talking, but I was dying to go over to Mimi's house. "Can I go and show Mimi? Please! Please! Pleeeaaase!!" Mom turned around and pointed to Mimi's front door. "She's not there. They left about an hour ago." Mimi's house looked dark—no lights were on. That meant . . . "They all left? To get the sister?" I asked. Mom nodded yes. I couldn't believe it! Mimi's big day was the same day as my big day? And we didn't even plan it that way. It was crazy unbelievable!

WHAT MR. SCRUFFERS IS VERY GOOD AT

Sniffing. I think she sniffed every single thing in our whole entire house. Mom said she was probably making a smell map of her new world. Dog brains have a whole different way of knowing about stuff than people's brains do. She can tell information about something by its smell. I use my eyes. I like my way better. I'm glad I don't have to sniff all the socks to tell which are mine.

Mr. Scruffers is also very good at sitting—if she thinks you have a treat in your hand—and at coming when you call her by her Mr.

Scruffers name. It's good that she's so smart, but bad that she likes that name.

WHAT ELSE MR. SCRUFFERS IS VERY GOOD AT

Mr. Scruffers is good at barking, especially when she sees a cat. When Mom said I could show Augustine Dupre my new dog, I didn't even think about anything except excitement. Since Augustine Dupre lives in the apartment in our basement it only took me about two seconds to get down there. I did my special knock on the door so that she would know it was me. I do this so that if Crinkles is visiting she doesn't have to shoo him away. Crinkles is really my neighbor Mrs. Luther's cat, but he's in love with Augustine Dupre so he spends a lot of time visiting with her. Before we got the dog Dad would not have been happy to know that Augustine Dupre had a cat in her apartment—even if it was just a sometimes cat. Before Mr. Scruffers, Dad had a No Animals in the House rule.

As soon as Augustine Dupre opened the door Mr. Scruffers went crazy! I couldn't see Crinkles but Mr. Scruffers must have smelled him.

WHAT IS HARD TO DO

It's really hard to talk in a normal voice if a dog is barking, a cat is hissing, and the person you are visiting is completely confused and upset. It is also really hard to know what to do when all these things are happening at the exact same time. The only good part was that I knew the exact right word to describe what was going on. It was chaos! We had just learned that word in school. It means crazy disorganized mess. It's one of those words that when you learn it you think, "I bet I'll never use this word in real life." But I had just learned it yesterday and here I was using it already. Miss Lois would have been impressed!

WHAT HAD NEVER HAPPENED BEFORE

"Sorry!" shouted Augustine Dupre, and she slammed her door right in my face. I had never had that happen before in my whole entire life. It was a surprise. It looks cool on TV, but when it happens to you in real life it feels kind of weird.

I could hear Augustine Dupre talking on the other side of the door. I guess she was upset because I couldn't understand a word she was saying. She talks in French when she is worked up about something. She was probably talking to Crinkles, trying to get him to stop hissing. I wonder if he could under-stand French? I had never thought about that before.

All the noise got Mom worried too, be-cause she stuck her head through the up-stairs door and shouted, "Is everything okay down there?" I was glad that Mr. Scruffers had stopped barking. "Yes, just excited, we're okay," I answered. "Well, don't bother Augustine Dupre for too long," said Mom, and she closed the door. I wasn't sure if we were ever going to be bothering Augustine Dupre again. Her door was still closed and we were just standing there waiting. Well, I was waiting. Mr. Scruffers was making pig snort noises and trying to push her nose under the door.

VERY IMPRESSIVE! I COULDN'T DO BETTER SNORTS IF I TRIED.

PIG ↑

After what seemed like forever, Augustine Dupre finally opened the door again. She squeezed through a little crack and then closed it behind her. She was keeping Crinkles in and Mr. Scruffers out.

WHAT YOU SHOULD NOT SAY AFTER YOU HAVE MADE SOMEONE'S LIFE SUDDENLY BE FILLED WITH CHAOS

"LOOK! I got a new dog! Isn't she cute!"

WHAT YOU SHOULD SAY INSTEAD

"I'm sorry. I forgot that Crinkles would be there. Is everything okay?"

I said both things to Augustine Dupre, only I said them in the wrong order. I couldn't help it. I was so excited about Mr. Scruffers.

WHAT AUGUSTINE DUPRE SAID

"Alors, c'est mignon, oui." I was worried it was something bad, but she smiled and bent down to give Mr. Scruffers some pets. If she had looked mad I wouldn't have asked her, but since she seemed okay I said, "What's that French thing you just said?" Augustine Dupre looked up. "Oh, I said, 'Yes, it is cute.' Your new dog is very cute!" She gave Mr. Scruffers a few more pets. "Is it a boy or a girl? What is its name?" The answer was not easy. It's the same sort of complicated I have with my Just Grace name—it's the kind of thing that always needs lots of explaining. I took a deep breath and said, "It's a girl, but her name is a boy name. It's Mr. Scruffers, but I'm going to change it as soon as I think of something really good."

Augustine Dupre didn't say anything for

minute and then she said, "How about Michou, or Fanette, or Amitee . . . There are so many lovely names, I'm sure you'll find one." She gave Mr. Scruffers one last pet and then stood up.

WHAT IS NOT GOING TO HAPPEN ANYMORE

I am not going to be sitting in Augustine Dupre's fancy apartment eating cookies with her and Mr. Scruffers. Augustine Dupre said that she thought it would be unfair to Crinkles if we let Mr. Scruffers into her apartment. I think she was worried that Crinkles would stop visiting her if he thought there was going to be a dog waiting there to chase him. This was probably the right thing to think. Augustine Dupre loves Crinkles as much as if he were her own cat. Of course she did not want to mess that up.

AUGUSTINE DUPRE IS KILLING MY LOVE FOR HER BY BEING WITH A DOG!!!

WHAT DAD SAID WHEN WE GOT BACK UPSTAIRS

Dad was waiting for us when we came back from our visit. "How did it go?" he asked. "Did Mr. Scruffers make a good impression?" I thought about it for a second and then said, "I guess okay. Augustine Dupre said she thought Mr. Scruffers was cute." "Well, good," said Dad. "I'm sure she just has to get used to us having a dog. I think she might be more of a cat person anyway. How about we get Mr. Scruffers set up for the night?" I didn't say anything, but I was pretty surprised about Dad knowing that Augustine Dupre liked cats. I wonder if he knew Crinkles visited her in her apartment.

WHAT IS NOT GOING TO WORK

Dad had done a lot of research about getting a new dog. He had a lot of dog facts. Mr. Scruffers had different feelings about Dad's facts.

DAD'S FACTS VS.
MR. SCRUFFERS'S FEELINGS

- Dogs like to feel safe.

- A dog crate is like a cozy, safe cave.

- It's a good idea to keep a new dog in a crate at night.

WHAT IS ONLY GOING TO WORK WHILE DAD IS IN THE ROOM

Dad pulled Mr. Scruffers's new pillow out of the crate and put it on the floor. "Dogs stay on the floor," he said, and he picked her up off my bed and put her on the pillow. "Good dog," said Dad. He put his hands on his waist, looked around, and then walked out of the room. If he were a superhero he would have said, "My job here is done!"

WHAT HAPPENED AS SOON AS DAD WALKED AWAY

Just like I was hoping, as soon as Dad left the room, Mr. Scruffers jumped right back on the bed. "Good dog," I said. It was exactly what I wanted—my new best friend to sleep right next to me.

WHAT I WAS SORRY ABOUT

It was too bad that Mimi wasn't home to do the bedtime light flashing. It would have been nice for us to share my first night with Mr. Scruffers together. It was dumb to flash my lights if she wasn't even at her window to see them. I hoped she was having fun with her new sister, and just when I thought that, I suddenly thought of something else: Sister has the same number of letters in it as new dog. Our flashes would spell out the new special things in our lives! It was another thing that was perfect.

1 2 3 4 5 6   1 2 3 4 5 6
NEW DOG SISTER

WHAT WAS NICE

Right before I went to sleep I looked up on my shelf and saw Chip-Up. It looked like he was looking down on us. "Thank you, Chip-Up." I whispered the words out loud, not because he could hear them, but more because I really, really meant them—it was kind of like a thank-you to the world.

WHAT I DID NOT EXPECT

Usually on Saturdays I get to sleep in. I don't get up until eight-thirty or sometimes even nine o'clock. I'm not a morning person.

What I did not know about Mr. Scruffers is that she is a morning dog.

At six a.m. she started jumping on and off the bed.

I pulled the covers over my head.

At ten minutes after six she started whimpering.

I stuck my head under the pillow.

At six-fifteen she started barking.

I had to get up.

WHAT I WAS NOT

Happy.

← MY SLEEPY FACE

WHAT I AM GLAD ABOUT

It's a good thing that we have a fenced yard, because it would not be exciting to stand around outside in your pajamas waiting for Mr. Scruffers to go to the bathroom. It takes her a long time to find the exact right spot. It was much better to be watching her through the window from inside the house.

WHAT IS TRUE

A cute dog wagging her tail at you can start to make you more of a morning person. When Mr. Scruffers came back inside we looked around for something to eat. I looked in the cupboards and she looked on the floor. I wasn't sure what she was supposed to have for breakfast. Dad hadn't told me that part yet. I got myself some cereal and milk. Sometimes on the weekends Mom makes pancakes or French toast, but I knew for sure that she was not going to be making either of these at six-thirty in the morning.

WHAT IS REALLY FUN

I was kind of glad that Mom and Dad were still sleeping or I would have never invented the cereal game. Turns out that Mr. Scruffers loves cereal. But, even more than just eating it she loves chasing it. At first I tried throwing pieces to her so she could catch them in her mouth, but she was terrible at catching. She didn't even know what to do.

CATCH IT,
MR. SCRUFFERS.

WHY IS SHE
THROWING CEREAL
AT ME?

I'm not the best thrower, so the times I missed her head she got all excited about chasing the cereal on the floor. That's how the game started. Mom and Dad would have definitely not been excited about me throwing cereal all over the house. But they were asleep and Mr. Scruffers was excellent at it, so they would never know.

WHAT IS AMAZING

You can get a ton of stuff done if you get up at six in the morning. By the time Mom and Dad came into the kitchen at eight-thirty, I had done a whole list of things already.

1. Played the secret cereal game with Mr. Scruffers.

2. Made a list of new dog names for Mr. Scruffers.

3. Played pull-the-sock with Mr. Scruffers until the sock was too slimy to touch anymore.

4. Made a nice Welcome sign for Mimi's front door.

5. Practiced walking Mr. Scruffers on the leash in the backyard.

I had used up so much energy that when Mom said, "Do you want me to make pancakes?" I said, "Yes. Yes I do." It was unusual, but true: I was hungry for a second breakfast.

WHAT IS NOT GOING TO BE EASY

After breakfast I got some treats for Mr. Scruffers so I could start training her for a new name. At first I tried Coco because it was one of my favorites. It was not Mr. Scruffers's favorite. She wouldn't even look at me when I called her that.

I tried the rest of the names, but it was the same thing. She acted like she couldn't even hear me. I even tried just Scruffers, because at least that was better than having the Mr. part, but it still didn't work. Miss Scruffers wasn't any better. It was hopeless. I was a sort of glad about that though, because Miss Scruffers is kind of hard to say.

Mr. Scruffers was sniffing the ground over at the fence. She didn't care one bit that I was trying to give her a beautiful new girl name. "Mr. Scruffers, you are totally impossible!" I shouted. I turned around and walked a couple of steps away. And then, when I looked down, there she was, standing right at my feet. She was there because she heard her name. She couldn't help it, and whether I wanted it or not she was probably going to stay Mr. Scruffers. "We're perfect for each other," I said, and I hugged her. "We both have dumb names."

WHAT I COULD NOT WAIT TO DO

Sometimes when you have a new thing it's fun to see how it feels to take that new thing to your old regular places. Some new things can make you feel completely different, but it depends on the new thing.

WHAT IS NOT SO EXCITING

Mom said I was not allowed to wander all over town by myself with Mr. Scruffers. I said going to the park was not wandering all over town, but she said Dad had to come with me.

I didn't want to hurt Dad's feelings, but the park was not going to be as much fun with him there. I was really wishing Mimi was back so she could come with me instead.

WHAT TURNED OUT TO BE GOOD

In the end it was good that Dad was with me. The park was filled with dogs. I was excited for Mr. Scruffers to meet them all. Everything was going perfectly fine until Mr. Scruffers met Bernie. As soon as she sniffed him, she turned crazy. She was barking and pulling, and pretty much everyone in the whole park was looking at us. I don't know why but she was 100 percent hating him.

Bernie is a nice little dog that Mimi, Sammy, Max, and I know really well. For a while we even had a job where we took him for walks. John, his owner, is also really nice, so it was doubly crazy that Mr. Scruffers was acting this way.

Dad had to pick up Mr. Scruffers and hold her just to get her to stop barking. I'm pretty sure everyone was happy that that worked. I'm really glad that we already knew John; otherwise the whole thing would have been even more embarrassing.

BERNIE

WHY IS THAT DOG BARKING AT ME?

ANOTHER GOOD THING

John said he and Bernie were on their way home, and as soon as they left the park Mr. Scruffers stopped being upset. Dad put her down and she was fine again. We were lucky about that. I'm glad she wasn't going to be hating every other dog in the world.

WHAT IS TRUE

Even though Mr. Scruffers was not perfect, I still loved her. It was only the second day of us being together, but I was sure that was not going to change.

On the way home Dad wanted to talk about what happened, probably to make sure that I was not mad at Mr. Scruffers, but I didn't need him to do that. I said, "I'm in love with Mr. Scruffers just the way she is." Dad seemed happy with that. "I'm glad," he said.

WHAT I WAS NOT EXPECTING WHEN I GOT HOME

Mimi's car was in the driveway. She was back! I couldn't believe it. I didn't think she would be home so soon. For a second I was disappointed that I didn't have a chance to stick my Welcome sign on her door, but that was only a small thing. Dad said he would take Mr. Scruffers into the house for a drink of water if I wanted to run over and see her right away. Of course I wanted to take Mr. Scruffers with me, but I could tell that he was not going to be letting me do that. He was probably worried that Mr. Scruffers would scare the new sister.

WHAT I WAS REALLY NOT EXPECTING

When I knocked on Mimi's door, Mimi's mom answered. She looked tired. Maybe the new sister was a baby. Babies were a lot of work. Mom said they pretty much made everybody tired. "Mimi is in her room," said her mom. "Maybe you can cheer her up." I raced up the stairs to see her. Maybe the baby had drooled on her. Babies did that too.

"MIMI!" I shouted. "I'm here! Guess . . . ?" I stopped my words. I wanted to tell her about

Mr. Scruffers and I wanted to ask about her new sister both at the same time—it was hard to decide which to do first. But Mimi was lying on her bed with her head down, and seeing her like that pushed both those thoughts right out of my brain. Something was not right. "What's wrong, Mimi?" I asked. "Are you okay?"

MIMI ON HER BED.

THE BIGGEST SURPRISE OF ALL

Mimi sat up. She had been crying. "The sister is not a sister!" she said, and then she started talking louder and louder until she was almost shouting. "The sister is not a girl! The sister is a BOY! I got a brother instead! I didn't get a SISTER!!!" My head was sitting on my neck like normal, but suddenly it felt all weird, like I could almost feel my brain trying to work. "What do you mean, you got a brother? What happened to the sister? Where did the sister go?" I had about a hundred questions. Mimi flopped herself back on the bed. "I can't talk about it," she mumbled.

I was 100 percent confused. Did she not want to talk about it, or was she not allowed to talk about it? Nothing was making any sense.

I couldn't decide what to do next. After a few minutes of watching Mimi I could tell that she was probably going to be staying lying down for a while. It was not comfortable to be standing there watching my best friend be sad and mad. I wanted to leave. "Uh, Mimi, I'm going to go, but I'll come back later," I said. "We can hang out then, okay? Okay, I'm going now. Bye." I was doing all the talking, but I couldn't just leave without saying anything. The whole thing was a mystery.

WHAT YOU DO WHEN YOU ARE COMPLETELY STUNNED, WHICH IS A GOOD WORD THAT MEANS SO SURPRISED YOU FEEL LIKE YOUR BRAIN CAN'T WORK

Usually when I leave Mimi's room I race down the stairs and Mimi's mom shouts, "Grace, be careful on the stairs!" This time it was different. My feet could hardly move. It was like my brain was using all its power to try to understand what Mimi had said, and there wasn't any left over for the regular stuff, like telling my legs how to walk.

LEGS CAN'T MOVE.

Maybe that's why Mimi's mom heard me. Or maybe it was because I was slower than usual. Or maybe she was waiting for me. I couldn't tell, but before I even got to the top of the stairs she came over tapped my shoulder and did the finger thing that means "Follow me."

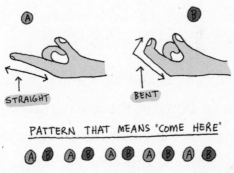

PATTERN THAT MEANS "COME HERE"

WHAT I SAW NEXT

Mimi's mom pointed to the new-sister room and made a shushing noise with her finger. Of course I was super curious. I tiptoed closer to have a look. There on the bed was a super-cute sleeping little boy. He was bigger than a baby, but not as big as Lily. Lily is a friend of ours who is four years old, so maybe he was not that old yet.

Mimi's mom touched my shoulder again and I followed her downstairs.

WHAT WAS A LITTLE UNCOMFORTABLE, BUT WORTH IT BECAUSE IT GAVE ME LOTS OF INFORMATION

Mimi's mom poured me a glass of apple juice and we sat down at the kitchen table together. It was weird. I had never done this with Mimi's mom before. We do not sit around just the two of us and talk. Ever!

WHAT MIMI'S MOM SAID

1. That Mimi was very upset. I already could tell this part.
2. That at almost the last minute the sister had not been able to be adopted.

3. That the brother needed a family, and that Mimi's mom had fallen in love with him after only ten minutes of meeting him.

4. That they were very lucky that the brother was able to come home with them so fast.

5. That he was three years old.

6. That his name was Robert.

WHAT I SAID

Mimi's mom was probably expecting me to say something important and good. Grown-ups are a lot better than kids at thinking of the exact right thing to say. I could tell that us being together and her telling me all this was special. It was the kind of moment your brain might remember for the rest of your life so it was important for me to say the right thing. Sometimes it's easier to think of all the

things you should probably not say instead of
the exact right perfect thing you should say.

WHAT I SHOULD NOT SAY

Usually I'm a fast thinker and I can make
the right words come out of my mouth so
fast that it might look like I didn't think about
them before I said them. This was not one
of those times. I was probably thinking too
long because Mimi's mom started talking
again. "Well, I just wanted you to know what
had happened," she said. "In case you could
help Mimi, you know, feel better about everything." Suddenly my empathy power was at

100 percent. "Don't worry," I said. "Mimi is going to love her new brother, and I am going to help her."

NORMAL PERSON WHO HEARS ABOUT SOMEONE BEING SAD.

GEE, THAT'S TOO BAD.

PERSON WITH EMPATHY POWER WHO HEARS ABOUT SOMEONE BEING SAD.

I HAVE TO DO SOMETHING TO HELP.

WHAT WAS A LITTLE UNCOMFORTABLE BUT STILL GOOD

Right when I stood up Mimi's mom came over and gave me a big hug. I had never hugged her before. She was squishier than Mom, but still it was nice. I think first hugs are probably always a little weird. "I'm so glad that Mimi has you," she said. Her voice was kind of sad—like almost crying—but when I looked up at her she was smiling. "Why don't you come by later," she said. "I'm going to make some of that banana bread you like." Mimi's mom's banana bread is the best! "Okay," I said. I waved goodbye and ran across the yard to my house.

WHAT I TOTALLY DIDN'T GET TO DO

I DIDN'T GET TO TELL MIMI ABOUT MR. SCRUFFERS!

WHAT HAPPENED AS SOON AS I WALKED IN THE DOOR

Mr. Scruffers went crazy with excitement. I couldn't believe how excited she was to see me. It was like I had been gone for days and she had been worried I was never coming home. It felt great to have her be so happy to see me. I could tell that she was feeling love for me as much as I was feeling love for her.

"Come on, Mr. Scruffers," I said. "Let's go." I ran up the stairs and she followed me right into my room.

THE NEW THINGS I WAS THINKING ABOUT

1. How I had to make a plan to help Mimi like her new brother.

2. How Mimi's brother had the same name as Robert Walters at school. And how that Robert had pretty much totally ruined the Robert name for me.

3. How to tell Mimi about my new thing when she was not at all excited about her new thing. And I was 100 percent

knowing for sure that if I did the telling in the wrong way, it was totally going to make her feel worse.

WHAT HELPS ME FEEL BETTER

This was a lot to think about. Sometimes when I am not feeling good it helps me feel better if I do a drawing—my favorite kind of drawings to do are comics. I like to tell silly stories, especially stories about teeny-tiny superpowers, because even a mini superpower is probably better than nothing.

NOT SO SUPER
BUT STILL GOOD

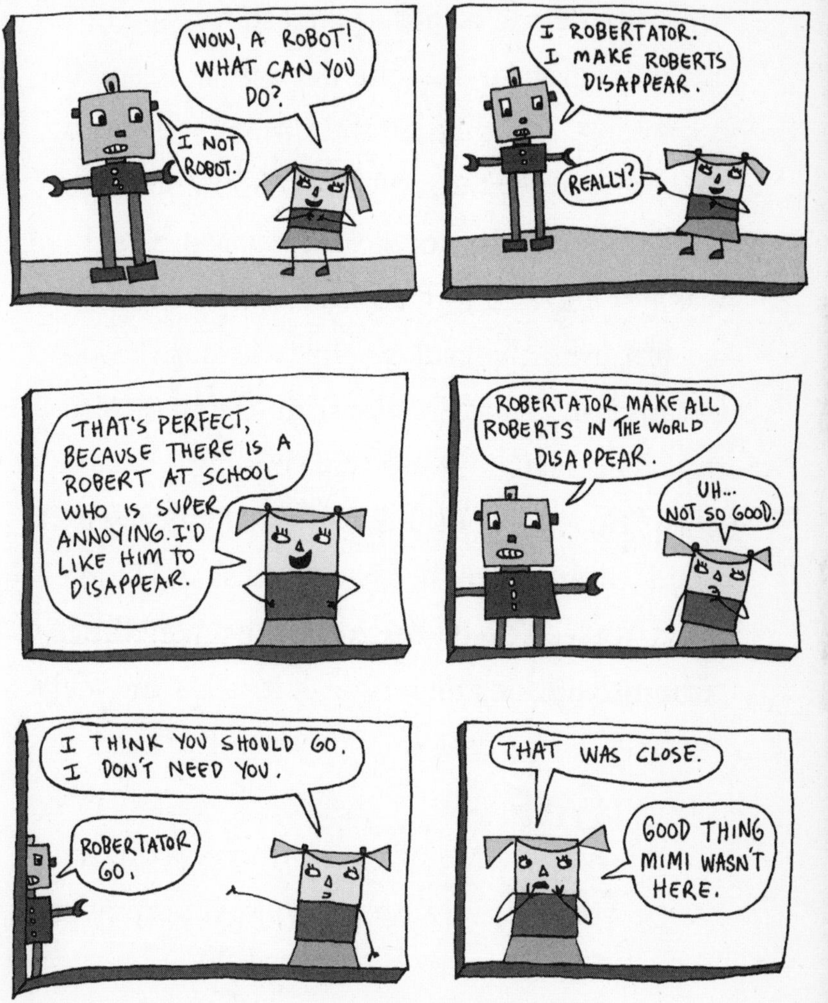

WHY IT CAN BE HARD TO EAT A GRILLED CHEESE SANDWICH

Mom made me a grilled cheese for lunch. I like it when she makes this because I can smell it cooking, and then by the time it's ready to eat, I am super hungry for it. Someone else was super hungry for it too, but Mom said I was not allowed to feed Mr. Scruffers any of it—not even the crusts. This was hard to do because Mr. Scruffers was sitting right next to my chair, watching me with big hungry dog eyes. "But Mom, I think she's really hungry," I said. Mom shook her head and said, "Don't do it. You can't feed her from the table. She'll turn into a monster."

For reasons I had never thought of before, being a dog owner can be really hard. I felt like every bite of sandwich I was taking was breaking Mr. Scruffers's heart.

After lunch Mr. Scruffers and I went out to the backyard to play fetch. I am spending a lot more time in my backyard than I ever used to before I got a dog. This is probably going to make me super healthy. Mr. Scruffers loves chasing games—they are her favorite. Mostly it's me doing the chasing and her doing the running away. She is fast and sneaky, which makes her hard to catch. She would have probably played for hours, but I had to take breaks and sit on the steps to rest.

WHAT I WAS NOT EXPECTING TO SEE

While I was resting I looked over and saw Augustine Dupre standing in her doorway. It seemed crazy, but it looked like she was wearing a supercape. When something is unusual a person who has a wondering-type brain cannot just say, "Hmm, oh well." A person with a wondering brain has to get up and go over and see what is going on.

"Hi! It's me!" I shouted, and waved as I walked closer. Maybe she was playing some kind of superhero game. I think that Augustine Dupre is a very interesting person, but seeing her in the cape made me  think that maybe she was even more interesting than I thought she was. When I got a little closer I could see that her supercape was really a towel.

WHAT AUGUSTINE DUPRE WAS NOT EXPECTING TO SEE

Me.

I could tell this because she kind of looked surprised. "Oh! My head is a mess," said Augustine Dupre. "I was just coloring my hair." Augustine Dupre never steps out of her door unless her clothes and her hair are perfectly perfect. I was a little disappointed that the towel/cape was not for something more exciting, but I didn't say that. Instead I said, "Oh, Mom colors her hair too."

After that I couldn't think of anything else to say. I could tell that Augustine Dupre was feeling uncomfortable, and just standing there was letting her uncomfortable feeling slowly creep over to my body too. I was glad when Mr. Scruffers started barking at something across the yard.

"I'm sorry, I have to go," I yelled, and I ran over to Mr. Scruffers. "Okay," said Augustine Dupre. When I looked back she was gone. It wasn't like seeing someone in their under-

pants, but somehow it felt like maybe it was a little bit the same.

WHAT TURNED OUT TO BE GOOD

I couldn't tell what Mr. Scruffers had been barking at. She had stopped by the time I got to her. We were just about to start a stick game when Mom called us in. "Mimi's mom just called to invite you over for some banana bread," said Mom. I looked down at Mr. Scruffers and Mom instantly read my mind. "No, you can't take her. I think Mimi should come here to meet Mr. Scruffers." Mom is super good at reading minds, especially when the answer starts with a no. It's not a power that I'm glad she has.

Mimi's new brother was probably going to be awake. I wanted to take him a present. I looked around my room, but there was nothing good that a little boy would like. Then suddenly I thought about Augustine Dupre and her supercape that wasn't really a supercape. It was perfect, and Mom only grumbled a little about me taking her brand-new dishtowel.

I made an R on the towel with some red tape that Mom has. It's my favorite tape because it's easy to rip and it doesn't try to stick to itself while you are using it.

TIE THIS TOP PART AROUND YOUR NECK.

WHAT WAS NOT GOOD

Mimi opened the door as soon as I knocked. I could tell she was still grumpy. She stomped up the stairs to her room and I followed her. As soon we got there she closed the door and started talking. She used a lot of words, but in the end, it came down to one big complaint.

WHAT MIMI SAID

1. Brothers are not as good as sisters.

I am not an expert on brothers or sisters so the only thing I could think of to say was "Well, maybe we should do some boy research and find out if that's true?" At school we had learned all about the scientific method. There are lots of rules about the right way to do experiments, but mostly what I was remembering was the other part Miss Lois had talked about. She'd said, "The best way to get answers to a question is to do research."

WHAT RESEARCH CAN DO

I was hoping that research was going to help answer some questions for Mimi.

Are sisters better than brothers?

Are brothers better than sisters?

Are they both the same?

But what I was mostly hoping for was this:

WHAT RESEARCH CANNOT DO

Research was probably not going to get Mimi's mom and dad to send the brother back, so I was hoping that sisters-are-better-than-brothers answer was not the one that was going to be true.

WHAT WAS SURPRISING

Just talking about it seemed to help make Mimi be in a better mood. She grabbed my hand and we went downstairs to the kitchen to get some banana bread. Mimi's mom and Robert were already sitting at the table. He looked pretty cute awake too. "Robert, this is Mimi's friend Grace," said Mimi's mom. "Hi, Robert." I smiled and waved at him. He looked up but didn't say anything. I think his mouth might have been too full of banana bread. As soon as Mimi's mom introduced me I suddenly remembered the book I had

made. I had 100 percent forgotten all about
it. At least I had the cape.

WHAT I WAS NOT EXPECTING

After our snack I showed Robert the supercape I had made for him. Mimi's mom said
she thought it was excellent, but I could tell
that Robert didn't even know what it was for.
I put it on and ran back and forth in the kitch-
en, but he just looked at me like I was crazy.
Finally Mimi said, "Here, let me show him." I
think she was worried that my feelings were
getting hurt. Mimi put the cape on and said,
"Look at me! I'm a superhero! Whoosh!"
and she ran off into the living room. Robert
jumped off his chair and ran after her. Mimi
ran back into the kitchen. Robert was close
behind her. "He likes chasing games, just like
Mr. Scruffers," I said. Mimi stopped suddenly.
"Who is Mr. Scruffers?"

Mimi gave Robert the cape while I started to talk.

WHAT I SAID NEXT

I'm pretty good about not saying it, because it's one of Dad's new big rules, but this was a once-in-a-lifetime occasion, plus I was way too excited to remember not to, so by accident I said, "OMG, Mimi! I got a dog!" Mimi froze like a statue. "A real dog? A real live dog?" asked Mimi. Then she was shouting. "Is it at your house? Can I see it? Is it big? Can we go! Let's go! Let's go NOW!"

ARMS WAVING IN THE AIR LIKE CRAZY.

WHAT HAPPENED NEXT

I ran out the door, Mimi ran out the door, and Robert ran out the door. We all raced across the front yard to my house. Mr. Scruffers was in the backyard, and I could hear her barking at something. "Let's go around the side," I shouted. I got to the side gate but suddenly no one was behind me. Then Mimi came walking up holding Robert's hand. "His legs are short," she said. "I couldn't leave him out front." I looked at Robert and then I had a thought. "Maybe you should pick him up. He might get scared." Mimi looked at Robert, and it looked like she was thinking about it too. "Okay," she said and she scooped him up. I wondered if she was happy about the being-able-to-carry-him part. It had been on her sister list, but I couldn't think about it anymore because Mr. Scruffers was going crazy on the other side of the fence and Mimi and Robert were ready to meet her.

WHO'S A GOOD DOG

Mr. Scruffers was so happy to see me that at first she didn't even pay any attention to Mimi or Robert. It was like she needed me to pet her before she could notice anyone else. When she finally ran over to meet Mimi, her tail was wagging. I was glad she chose that instead of barking. Robert was squirming around like crazy in Mimi's arms. I couldn't tell if he was scared or if he wanted to get down. Finally she had to put him down or she probably would have dropped him.

WHAT WAS UNEXPECTED

Robert took off after Mr. Scruffers and started chasing him all over the yard. Robert was squealing and having the greatest time. I think Mr. Scruffers was liking it too, but I wasn't totally 100 percent sure how much.

Watching them, I suddenly had a question. "Mimi, does Robert talk?" Mimi shrugged and said, "Mom says he does, but I haven't heard him yet. I don't think he likes to do it if anyone is around." And then she asked me a question. "Are you sad you got a boy dog, because remember, you really wanted a girl dog?" Mimi was right. *Girl dog* was on my list of dog-must-haves.

WHAT I SAID NEXT WITHOUT THINKING

"Mr. Scruffers *is* a girl—she just came with a boy name. I tried to change it, but it's not as easy as I thought it would be. She likes being called Mr. Scruffers."

WHAT I WAS SUDDENLY THINKING

Was that the wrong thing to say? Did Mimi ask me that question because she is sad about Robert being a boy? Is she going to think I'm lucky and she is not?

WHAT MIMI SAID

"Really? Mr. Scruffers is a girl? Wow." She was looking at Robert and Mr. Scruffers racing around. "How about Mrs. Scruffers? Can you change it to that?" Mimi is a good problem solver. She always thinks of the easiest way to fix something first—not everyone is like that. I shook my head no. "I already tried that," I said. "She only comes, or even looks at you, if you use her whole Mr. Scruffers name."

Suddenly Mimi started laughing. I couldn't tell what was so funny. She completely had the giggles. It's a weird feeling to be standing next to someone who is laughing and to have no idea what they are laughing about. When this happens one of these two things can happen.

WHAT HAPPENED TO ME

I started smiling and laughing too, and I had ab-
solutely no idea why. Mimi was trying to talk
but she could hardly get the words out. The
more she tried, the more she laughed. Finally I
was able to figure out what she was saying.

THAT'S ... LIKE ... IF ... ROBERT ...
WAS ... HA, HA, HA, ... CALLED ...
HA, HA, HA, GERALDINE ... HA, HA, HA,
OR ROBERTA ... HA, HA, HA!

We were both laughing like crazy. It was
silly and funny and the more she laughed the
more I laughed. It felt like the old Mimi was back.

WHAT CAN STOP LAUGHING IN A SECOND

"Mimi funny." Mimi and I both heard it, but
we were not watching to see who said it. It
was either Mr. Scruffers or Robert, because

they were both standing there looking at us. Either way it was the kind of thing that we knew we had to pay attention to. "What did you say?" asked Mimi. She was looking at Robert. I guess she had pretty much decided it hadn't been Mr. Scruffers. Robert looked at her, but he didn't say it again.

"Mimi, he said your name!" I knew this was important. "Good job," said Mimi, and she patted him on the head. She was still smiling from all the laughing. "Let's go inside," I said. I was suddenly thirsty and hungry. Mr. Scruffers ran to the door. She was probably thirsty too.

WHAT WAS NICE

Obviously Mom had been waiting for us to come in. She had drinks, fruit, and cookies all set out on the table waiting for us. I like it when she is in her supermom mode.

THERE IS FRUIT, COOKIES, AND THREE KINDS OF BEVERAGES.

SNACK BAG WITH MORE SNACKS

"Sit here," said Mimi. She pulled out a chair and helped Robert sit down. "His name is Robert," I told Mom. I had already kind of gotten used to his name and was hardly even thinking about Robert Walters anymore when I said it. This was good—doing lots of thinking about Robert Walters was not something I wanted.

WHAT I NOTICED

Mr. Scruffers sat on the floor next to Robert. At first I was sad because I thought maybe it meant she liked him more than me—and she had just met him. I wanted her to sit next to me. But then after a few minutes I knew it was only because she was smart. Robert dropped way more crumbs than anyone else.

WHAT CAN GO BY SUPER FAST

A Saturday that is filled with new things.

After the snack Mimi and Robert had to go home. Mr. Scruffers and I went upstairs to rest and play.

WHAT MR. SCRUFFERS DOES NOT LIKE

Accessories.

GRRRR

WHAT HAPPENED AT NIGHT

I was so tired, I wanted to go to bed before nine o'clock. Usually I try to get Mom and

Dad to let me stay up later on the weekends, but tonight I just wanted to sleep. I guess that's what happens when you get up at six in the morning. I let Mr. Scruffers out one last time and then we went upstairs. I flashed my lights for Mimi but she was probably still up watching TV or something because she didn't flash back at me.

Before I go to sleep at night I like to think about all the things that have happened in my day, but tonight the only thought I had was *I hope Dad doesn't make Mr. Scruffers get off the bed while I am sleeping,* and then I must have fallen asleep, because I don't remember anything else.

WHAT I HAD TO DO FIRST THING IN THE MORNING

A project can be fun if you have the idea in your head about how to do it. If you are confused about the how-to-do-it part the fun can turn into worry instead.

MY PROJECT

Find out if brothers are good. Find out more about boys.

HOW TO DO IT

WHAT I NEEDED TO HAVE FOR BREAKFAST

I like to have French toast when I am really using my empathy powers. I don't know why it helps, but somehow it makes my brain think that everything will turn out all right. I was lucky that it was Sunday. Mom doesn't like to make French toast on school days.

WHAT ELSE I WAS LUCKY ABOUT

Mr. Scruffers did not get up until seven-thirty. That was still early for a weekend, but it wasn't as bad as yesterday, and for that I was glad.

WHAT CAN HAPPEN

Just because you have a special breakfast, and you really, really, really want to think of a good idea, it doesn't mean that it will happen.

I wanted to go over and see Mimi because being next to her and Robert might be a good way to get ideas, but Mom said I was not allowed to interrupt them until ten o'clock. I didn't think it could happen, but even though Mr. Scruffers was with me I was still suddenly bored. I did not feel like drawing, playing with the dog, reading, or any of the other things I normally like to do. All I could think of was that it was nine-thirty-five and I still had twenty-five more minutes to wait.

WHAT HAPPENED AT TEN A.M.

I left Mr. Scruffers in the backyard and ran across to Mimi's house. I was kind of excited to see Robert. I wanted to give him the book I had made. Mimi's dad opened the door. He was holding Robert. I was not expecting that so it took me a minute to think of what to say. In the end I just said, "Hi," and handed him the book. "Is this for me?" asked Mimi's

dad. "I was looking for a new book to read."
I could tell that he was joking. "I made it for
Robert," I said. This part was not really true
but I didn't want to say, "I made it for the new
sister, but since Mimi didn't get a new sister I
figured I could give it to Robert instead, and
even though he is a boy and not a girl, he will
probably still like it anyway." That was a lot
to say, and just in case Robert could understand all those words, I didn't want him to
feel bad that I was giving him someone else's
present.

Mimi's dad smiled and said, "Thank you,
Grace. This is so nice of you," and then he
showed Robert the book. "Look, son. This
is for you." I hadn't thought of Robert being
a son, so that was kind of cool. Mimi's dad
pointed to the kitchen and said, "Mimi's in
there. Robert and I are just going to put on
our shoes."

WHAT WAS NOT GREAT

Mimi and her mom were in the kitchen packing up snacks for the day. "We're going shopping and then on a picnic," said Mimi. She seemed grumpy again. "That doesn't sound bad," I said. "Furniture shopping!" complained Mimi. "Oh," I said, and then because Mimi's mom was looking the other way I stuck out my tongue. Furniture shopping was the worst! I was glad I made Mimi smile.

POOR YOU.

"We're going to get Robert some boy furniture for his room," said Mimi's mom. "Mimi is going to help be the designer. It'll

be fun." Mimi did not look like she thought it was going to be fun. "The only good part is the picnic," said Mimi. "We're having egg salad sandwiches." I wanted to stick my tongue out again, but that would have been rude. Mimi and I are best friends and we like a lot of things the same, but eggs is not one of them!

"When are you going?" I asked. "As soon as we get our shoes on," said Mimi's mom. This was another reason to stick my tongue out. I turned my head and did it just for me, because now I was like Mimi—unhappy. Now I couldn't watch her and Robert to get ideas.

WHAT I SHOULD HAVE EXPECTED

After Mimi left, which was about three minutes later, I went back home. It was a good thing too, because Mr. Scruffers was barking like crazy. I thought that maybe it was a squirrel, but when I got into the backyard I saw that it was Crinkles. Crinkles was on the picnic table with all his fur fluffed up and he was growling at Mr. Scruffers. Those two were not going to get along at all. I'm sure Crinkles was on his way to visit with Augustine Dupre.

Dad says it's never safe to get in the middle of a dogfight or a catfight. I was guessing the same was true for a dog-and-cat-almost-fight. I tried calling Mr. Scruffers away, but she acted like she couldn't hear me, and maybe she couldn't with all the barking she was doing. She was making a lot of noise. Dad finally came outside and said, "What in the Sam Pete is going on out here?" I pointed at the table.

THE I-DON'T-LIKE-DOGS POSE

WHAT DOGS DO

I think dogs listen to dad voices better than they listen to daughter voices. At least Mr. Scruffers does. As soon as Dad yelled her name Mr. Scruffers rolled on her back and put her legs in the air. Dad says that's her way of saying, "Okay, you can be the boss."

He walked over and picked her up. Crinkles must have thought that Dad was the boss too, because as soon as Dad got close

he jumped off the picnic table and ran away.
"I don't know why that cat would come into
the yard when there's a dog here," said Dad.
I didn't say anything but I knew the answer.
It was Augustine Dupre. It was love.

I WILL BE
BRAVE. THAT DOG
WON'T STOP ME. I
MUST SEE MY
TRUE LOVE.

WHAT TURNED OUT OKAY

I thought that I was going to hate every minute of Mimi being gone, but instead I found
something that took up my whole day without me even noticing it.

I worked on my map.

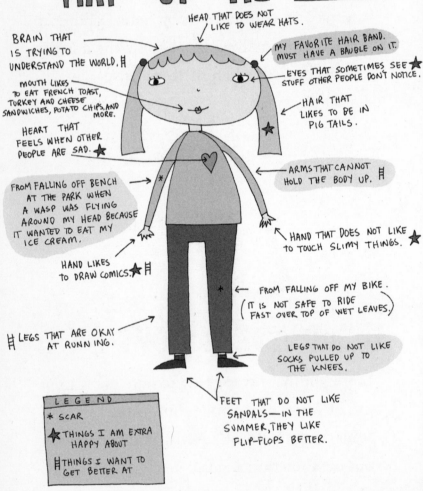

MAP OF ME
GRACE S.

HEAD THAT DOES NOT LIKE TO WEAR HATS.

BRAIN THAT IS TRYING TO UNDERSTAND THE WORLD. ⧓

MY FAVORITE HAIR BAND. MUST HAVE A BAUBLE ON IT.

EYES THAT SOMETIMES SEE STUFF OTHER PEOPLE DON'T NOTICE. ★

MOUTH LIKES TO EAT FRENCH TOAST, TURKEY AND CHEESE SANDWICHES, POTATO CHIPS, AND MORE.

HAIR THAT LIKES TO BE IN PIG TAILS.

HEART THAT FEELS WHEN OTHER PEOPLE ARE SAD. ★

ARMS THAT CANNOT HOLD THE BODY UP. ⧓

FROM FALLING OFF BENCH AT THE PARK WHEN A WASP WAS FLYING AROUND MY HEAD BECAUSE IT WANTED TO EAT MY ICE CREAM.

HAND THAT DOES NOT LIKE TO TOUCH SLIMY THINGS. ★

HAND LIKES TO DRAW COMICS. ★ ⧓

FROM FALLING OFF MY BIKE. (IT IS NOT SAFE TO RIDE FAST OVER TOP OF WET LEAVES.)

⧓ LEGS THAT ARE OKAY AT RUNNING.

LEGS THAT DO NOT LIKE SOCKS PULLED UP TO THE KNEES.

FEET THAT DO NOT LIKE SANDALS—IN THE SUMMER, THEY LIKE FLIP-FLOPS BETTER.

LEGEND
* SCAR
★ THINGS I AM EXTRA HAPPY ABOUT
⧓ THINGS I WANT TO GET BETTER AT

I only stopped for lunch and to take Mr. Scruffers for a walk with Mom. I even let Mom hold the leash. That made her really happy. She said the last time she held a dog on a leash was when she was a teenager. It's hard to imagine her as a teenager—my brain just can't do it. My brain can only imagine the exact same Mom, only shorter.

MOM
TODAY

MOM
TEENAGER

WHAT WAS LUCKY

It was good we didn't run into Bernie on our walk. Mom would not have been so excited about that.

THE PERFECT TIME TO SAY TA-DA

Mom was loading up the dishwasher from dinner—I don't have to help on Sundays, so I ran upstairs to get my map. I couldn't wait to show her. I jumped into the kitchen doorway and shouted out "TA-DA!!" super loud. "Ahh!" Mom screamed, and dropped the plate she was holding. I had 100 percent surprised her. Lucky for her the plate didn't break. "Goodness, Grace! Do you have to yell?" "Yes, yes, I do," I said, and I waved my map in the air. If you spend an entire day doing homework and not complaining, I think you should get to yell about being happy when you are done.

Mom must have thought so too, because instead of getting angry she said, "Well, congratulations, then."

WHAT WAS A GOOD ENDING TO THE DAY

Even though I didn't get to see Mimi during the day it was nice that we at least got to flash our lights at each other before bed. One day it would be fun if she waved with Robert and I waved with Mr. Scruffers, but I knew she was probably not ready to be wanting to do that yet. Her love for Robert was not like my love for Mr. Scruffers. People love maybe took longer than animal love.

TWO NICE THINGS

1. Dad came in to say good night and he did not even say one word about Mr. Scruffers being on the bed.

2. Mr. Scruffers solved the cat-near-Mimi problem before it could even start. Mimi would not have to worry about her brother being a furball. Mr. Scruffers would keep Crinkles away.

WHAT WAS A SURPRISE THE NEXT DAY

Mr. Scruffers got me up at seven-fifteen. This was the perfect time for a school day. Instead of letting her out in the backyard, I put on my shorts and went to the front yard. I wanted to be there in case Mimi wanted to visit with me. She can't see our backyard from inside her house.

Mr. Scruffers was pulling on her leash like crazy. I was thinking that maybe she smelled squirrel, but it wasn't a squirrel. It was Sammy Stringer. He was standing at the edge of our driveway with all his newspapers on his bike. "Is that yours?" he asked. He was pointing at Mr. Scruffers. Unfortunately Mr. Scruffers was pooping right when he said that. With a normal person you would not have to think about your answer to the question—you would just say, "Yes, this is my new dog, Mr. Scruffers." But with Sammy it was more complicated. Sammy had a thing about poop, and this made my brain confused for a minute.

"What's its name?" asked Sammy. This was a big clue to my brain's question. "Her name is Mr. Scruffers," I said, and then in my brain I counted, one one thousand, two one thousand, three one thousand, and then I pointed at Sammy and waited for the question. "Why does she have a boy name?" asked Sammy. It was perfect timing and exactly the question I was expecting.

Being right made me smile. "She just came that way," I said. "Someone else already picked her name. I wanted to think of a girl name—" "Hey, I know," said Sammy, suddenly interrupting me. "What about Wanda? Call her that. Wanda's a great girl name."

Sammy is not one of those people who understands the word *no* very well, so we had to try out the Wanda name right then and there so he could understand that it was not going to work.

SAMMY STANDING BACK, HE DOESN'T REALLY LIKE DOGS.

WANDA! WANDA! LOOK HERE. WANDA!

MR. SCRUFFERS NOT EVEN LOOKING AT ME.

I was glad about that because even though it was weird, I was kind of getting used to the Mr. Scruffers name.

WHAT I DID THAT WAS SURPRISING

Sammy is not anywhere near my best friend, but for some reason while we were standing there my mouth just couldn't stop talking. I told him all about Mimi, about the new sister being a brother, about how I was feeling bad for Mimi and how I wanted to help her know more about boys and brothers so she could maybe feel better. I told him everything, and I didn't even think about what I was saying before I said it. It was like he had the same pow-ers as Augustine Dupre only I had never noticed it before. Were they both super listeners?

SAMMY

AUGUSTINE DUPRE

* PRONOUNCED "MWA OSSI" IT MEANS "ME TOO"!

WHAT SAMMY SAID

As soon as I finished talking Sammy said, "Wait here!" and he ran over to his bike. He came back with a long, skinny paper tube. "You can borrow this until school starts," he said. "It's my Map of Me. Mimi can study it so she can know more about being a boy." Sometimes when something surprising happens it's hard to know exactly what the right thing to say is.

All I could think of to say was "Wow." "I know," said Sammy, and then he turned around and ran back to his bike. "I have to finish delivering my papers," he shouted. He jumped on his bike and in two seconds he was gone. I couldn't see him anymore, but I could hear him. "Don't forget to bring it to school, and don't get spaghetti on it," he yelled. Sammy is one of those people who always leaves you with a question in your brain.

WHAT I AM NOW CURIOUS AND SCARED OF

FACTS

1. Sammy made a Map of Me.
2. Sammy likes weird, gross things.
3. Yellow rubber gloves are made to keep your hand skin safe from touching weird, gross things.
4. Sometimes dogs like to eat weird, gross things. It would be bad if Mr. Scruffers ate Sammy's map.
5. Explaining yellow rubber gloves and Sammy's map to Mom would take a long time.

All these are the reasons why I decided to open Sammy's map in the bathroom. It

was the one place where I could be alone
and no one was going to ask me anything ab-

out what I was doing. All
I had to do was sneak in
the yellow gloves.

SAMMY'S MAP OF ME

Mostly I was happy that there was nothing
yucky attached to the map. I didn't need the
gloves after all. Sammy's map was made with
words and pictures, just like mine, only it was
completely different.

SOMETIMES WHEN YOUR BRAIN IS OVERLOADED WITH INFORMATION OR FEELINGS THERE IS ONLY ONE THING YOU CAN SAY

After reading Sammy's map I just stood
there and thought, *Wow.*

MAP OF SAMMY STRINGER

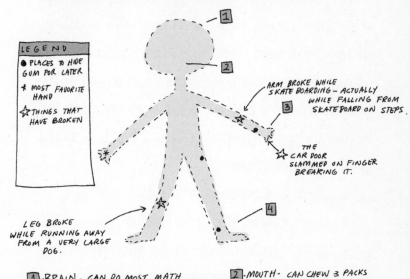

LEGEND
- ● PLACES TO HIDE GUM FOR LATER
- ✱ MOST FAVORITE HAND
- ☆ THINGS THAT HAVE BROKEN

1
2

ARM BROKE WHILE SKATEBOARDING — ACTUALLY WHILE FALLING FROM SKATEBOARD ON STEPS.

3

THE CAR DOOR SLAMMED ON FINGER BREAKING IT.

LEG BROKE WHILE RUNNING AWAY FROM A VERY LARGE DOG.

4

1 - BRAIN - CAN DO MOST MATH PROBLEMS WITHOUT PAPER.
- KNOWS ANIMAL POOP! CAN TELL WHAT KIND OF ANIMAL DID IT JUST BY LOOKING AT THE SCAT.*
* SCIENTIST NAME FOR POOP

2 - MOUTH - CAN CHEW 3 PACKS OF GUM AT ONCE.
- FAVORITE FOOD SPAGHETTI
- DOES NOT LIKE SALAD
- CAN BLOW A BUBBLE AS BIG AS MY HEAD

3 - HANDS - THINGS MY HANDS HAVE TOUCHED
- POOP, MARBLES, DIRT, WORMS, CAR ENGINE, OIL, FOOD, DEAD BIRD, FEATHERS, GRASS, TREES, OCEAN, RIVER, LAKE, ROCK, MUD, FISH
✱ 1 THING I WANT TO TOUCH - VOLCANO
✱ 1 THING I DO NOT WANT TO TOUCH - ANIMALS

4 - FEET - COUNTRIES MY FEET HAVE BEEN IN:
U.S.A., MEXICO, CANADA
- CANNOT DANCE
- LIKE TO WEAR SHOES
- LIKE TO STAND ON THINGS WITH WHEELS

THE ONE THING I WAS KNOWING RIGHT AWAY

Sammy's Map of Me was not going to help Mimi love Robert more. In fact, it might even scare her. It was too much boy information, or maybe it was just too much Sammy-kind-of-boy information. It was like my picture book project for Robert—it was going to be better to leave most of it out. The facts that I could tell her were . . .

1. Boys like to collect things.
2. Boys can be silly and funny.
3. Boys can be thoughtful. (Sammy letting me look at his map was proof of this.)
4. Boys have lots of imagination.

This was not an amazing list, and Mimi probably knew all this already.

WHAT WAS SURPRISING

It was harder to sneak the gloves and the map

out of the bathroom than it was to sneak them into it. Both Mr. Scruffers and Dad were right there when I came out. "Oh, good," said Dad. "Your mom sent me to look for you. It's time for breakfast." Unfortunately Mr. Scruffers immediately started jumping all over me like she hadn't seen me in a million years and I dropped the rubber gloves.

"What are those for?" asked Dad. It's a good thing I'm a fast thinker. "It's an experiment . . . for school," I said. "Okay, well, come eat your breakfast first," he said. And then suddenly on the way to the table I thought of a new fact for the list.

5. Boys do not ask a lot of questions.

WHAT WOULD HAVE HAPPENED IF MOM SAW ME COME OUT OF THE BATHROOM

I was super glad it had been Dad instead.

WHAT WAS UNUSUAL

Usually I go to Mimi's house to get her for our walk to school, but today she came over before I was even ready. I put Sammy's map inside my map so she wouldn't see it. I didn't want to show it to her if I didn't have to.

Today was a big day for Mr. Scruffers. It was the first day I was going to be gone. Mom and Dad promised to give her lots of attention so she wouldn't be sad. It was hard to say goodbye. I could tell she wanted to come with me. Mimi had a new goodbye too, but she was not as sad about hers as I was about mine.

On the way to school Mimi had lots to say about her shopping adventure. I was glad about that—it made me not think about Mr. Scruffers as much. Mimi said that Robert was loving the new bed she picked for him. "It looks like a rocket ship," she said. "It's a perfect boy bed!" I think it was a good sign that she was doing empathy thinking for Robert.

WHAT WAS A SURPRISE AT SCHOOL

Mr. Frank was back. Miss Lois said that he was going to stay until Friday because he wanted to see our finished maps and he had a special project to tell us about. I was getting the feeling that Mr. Frank was in love with thinking up project ideas. With everyone excited and talking about Mr. Frank, I was able to give Sammy his map back without almost anyone noticing—anyone except for Robert Walters.

"Hey! What's that?" asked Robert. "Is it a giant love note?" I glared at him. I wished my eyes had zapping powers to make him disappear, or do something he'd be sorry about.

Even though I tried really hard, nothing happened. He was still there bugging me.

"Love note, love note, love note." Robert moved his mouth like he was singing the words.

"Robert, please turn around. One more strike and you'll be out." Miss Lois's words worked like magic. She was for sure loving her new plan.

WHAT HAPPENED TO ME NEXT

WHY THIS WAS TOO BAD

I didn't want to be in a bad mood, but I couldn't help it. Sometimes it's like that. Even though you don't want to be there in the bad mood, you can't change it—you're there, and you're stuck! Maybe that is why when Mr. Frank said that we were all going to be doing a project involving comics I felt worse instead of better. My bad mood had changed even one of my most favorite things.

IF I WERE IN A GOOD MOOD

BECAUSE OF MY BAD MOOD

Comics are my thing.

WHAT IS ACTUALLY GOOD

It's a good thing that I don't have laser eyes or I would have completely fried Robert's brain with all the "GRRRRRR" looks I was giving him.

WHAT WAS FINALLY HERE

Recess!

Sometimes moving around can help unhappy feelings go away. Mimi and I walked outside. "Aren't you excited about the comic thing?" she asked. I think she was trying to cheer me up. "No!" I said it in a real grumpy voice. I was in a bad mood and it was all Robert's fault. I crossed my arms and made a big sigh. "If everyone does comics, they won't be special. I should just stop making them."

"What?" asked Mimi. I could tell she was confused. "No one does comics like you. You love them, and you're so good at them. You can't stop. I thought for sure you'd be happy that more people were going to try making some. More people doing and reading comics is a good thing."

I was thinking about what she was saying when she started talking again.

WHAT MIMI SAID NEXT

"It's like Roberts," said Mimi. "In all the world there are good Roberts and not-so-good Roberts. If you want people to be nice to any of the Roberts, you really need the good Roberts to be around. If you don't have enough good Roberts, then people start to think that all Roberts are bad, and they won't be nice to them—even if they meet a friendly one. The good ones are really important. The more good ones the better."

THE ROBERT STORY

Mimi stopped for a second and then she said, "That's why we have to help my brother be a good Robert." Then she looked at the ground like she was embarrassed or maybe like she couldn't believe what she had just said. It was true. She had said something pretty big. It was surprising to both of us. She had used the words "my brother" for the first time ever. It's the kind of thing that most people wouldn't have noticed, but a best friend is different. I knew it was special. Mimi was making her love change from sister love to brother love. "Oh, Mimi," I said, and I put my arms around her. "You are . . . Wow!"

AND THEN

Mimi and I spent the whole rest of recess smiling—we couldn't help it. Sammy saw us and said, "It worked, right?" Mimi looked confused. "Yes, it was good," I said. "Okay, you should try Glenda next. That's a good girl name. See ya." He did a half wave and was gone. It was nice. Sammy was easy. He asked hardly any questions and seemed perfectly happy with a fast answer. I looked at Mimi. I was not thinking the same thing about her. She was complicated. She was a girl. She was always going to be full of questions, and I could tell that she was thinking of about a hundred of them right now. It was going to take a while to get them all answered and explain everything.

But that was not my biggest thought. My really big thought was one I had never had before. It was about Robert. Mimi and I are girls. We are not easy. Poor Robert. Was *he* going to be able to handle us?

THE BEST WHAT HAPPENED LATER

Mimi and I found the perfect way to end our day. I'm hoping that even when I get old and my brain gets filled up with all sorts of other things that I will still remember it, because there was one thing I was knowing. It was special.

SIX PERFECT FLASHES!

BOOK 8

WHAT GRACE WILL BE THINKING ABOUT IN HER NEXT BOOK